A Number Slumber

Suzanne Bloom

BOYDS MILLS PRESS

AN IMPRINT OF HIGHLIGHTS

Honesdale, Pennsylvania

To Noah and Jesse, my shining sons
—SB

Text and illustrations copyright © 2016 by Suzanne Bloom

Boyds Mills Press
An Imprint of Highlights
815 Church Street
Honesdale, Pennsylvania 18431
boydsmillspress.com
Printed in China

ISBN: 978-1-62979-557-7
Library of Congress Control Number: 2015958455

First edition
Production by Sue Cole
The text is set in Buckley.
The illustrations are done in pastel.

10 9 8 7 6 5 4 3 2 1

What do you do to get ready for bed?

Do you brush
your teeth?

Have a story read?

Do you put your jammies on before

or after you start to yawn?

Once you're tucked in
warm and snug,
do you ask for
one more hug?

What do **other** sleepyheads do when their busy day is through?

Ten terribly tired tigers

tiptoe to their beds.

Nine normally nimble newts

rest their sleepy heads.

Eight exhausted elephants

curl up with their trunks.

Seven slightly stinky skunks somersault

into their bunks.

Six slumbering sun bears

snuggle in a heap.

Five frisky foxes

finally fall asleep.

Four flamingos flop

and close their little eyes.

Three throaty thrushes

warble lullabies.

TWO tuckered turtles

tuck themselves in tight.

One really weary wombat

yawns . . .

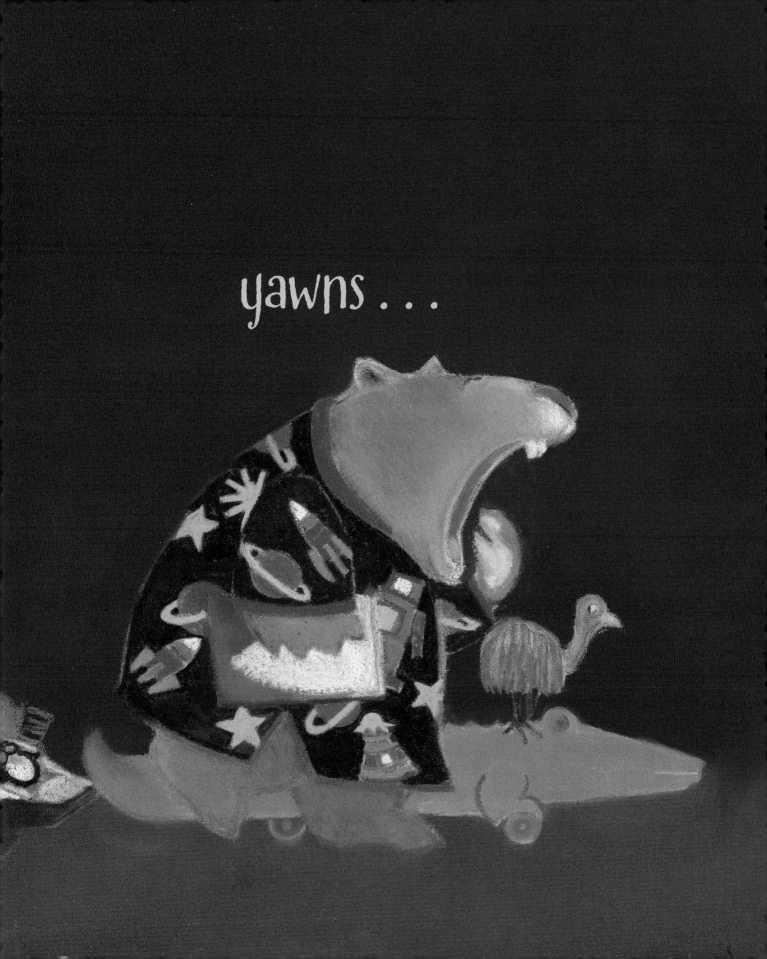

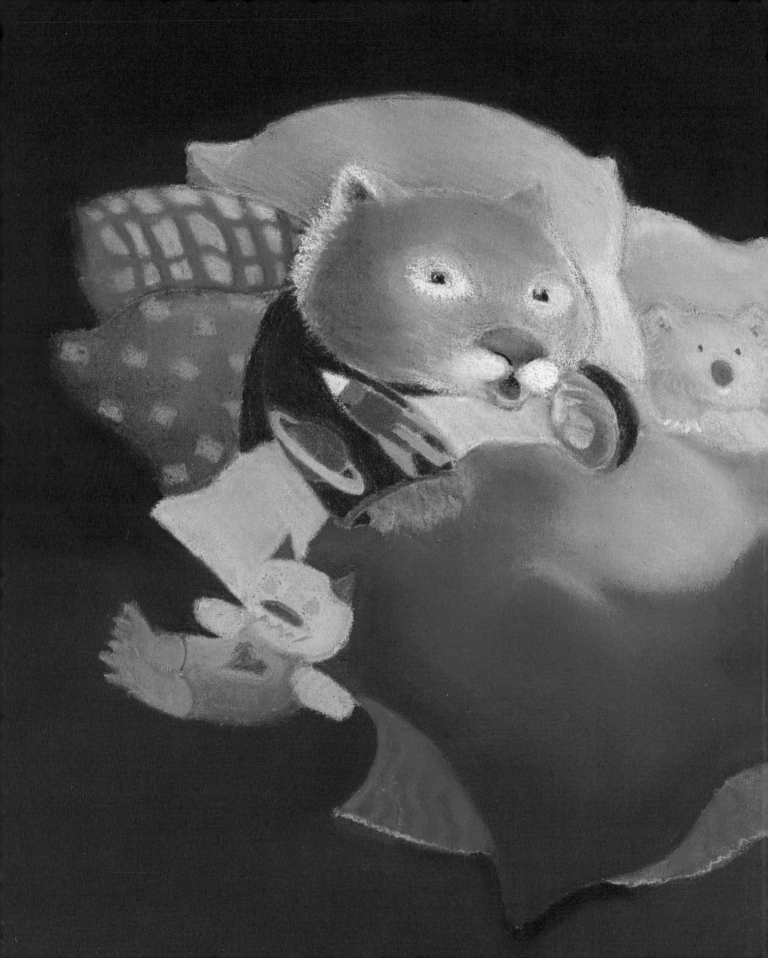

and whispers "nighty-night."

What do **other** sleepyheads do?

Fall fast asleep,
just like you.

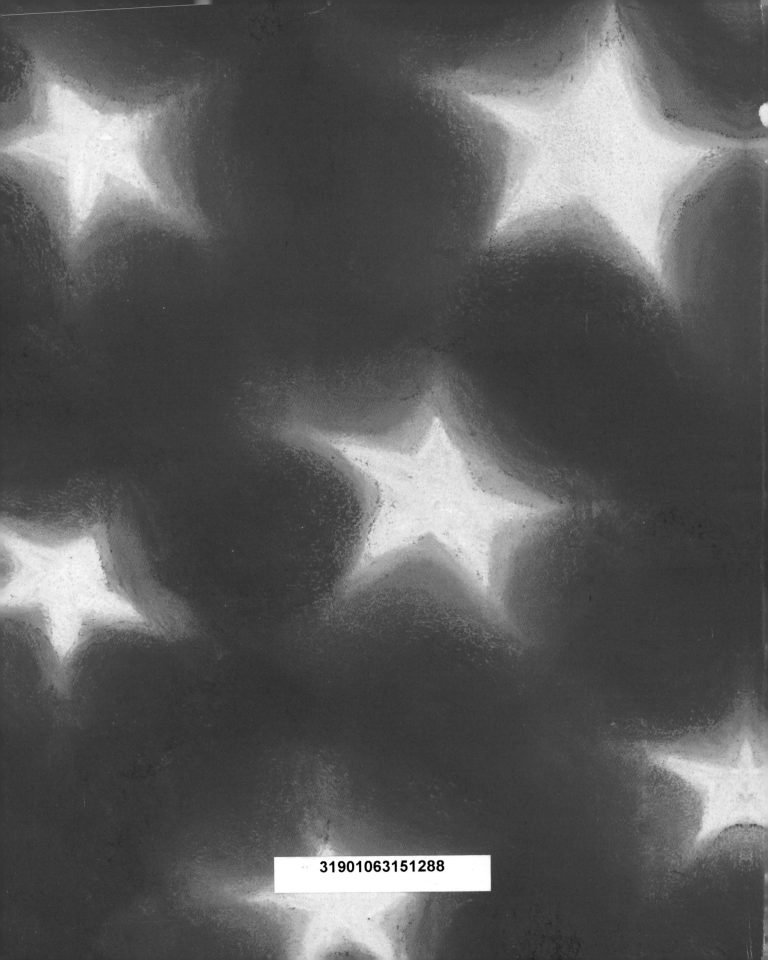